TALES FROM THE PUZZLE STORE

RICHARD FREEBORN

For Jackie

INTRODUCTION

You know how your footsteps echo in those concrete stairwells that lead from the parking lot to the inside of the building and make you wonder if someone else is in there with you?

Between Christmas 2020 and New Year's 2021, I had that experience. As I reached the landing midway between floors, I looked up to find the other person there. No-one. Then I looked down.

Lying close to the railing and almost hidden in the covering of dust and grime was a single lonely piece from a jigsaw puzzle.

My first thought was how upset someone was going to be when they finished the puzzle and found a piece missing. It's happened to me. A single missing piece shouldn't stop you from seeing the overall picture but does.

My second thought was, "Don't touch it!"

I wasn't worried about contamination or exposure to something contagious.

Inside my head was the idea that once I touched the

puzzle piece, it would transport me into another world or dimension, and that remote watcher I imagined I'd heard in the stairwell above would claim another victim.

"Senior moment?" my wife asked with raised eyebrows as she stepped round me and onto the second flight up, her flip-flops echoing up and down the stairwell.

I followed her, and in my head the piece of jigsaw followed me.

Suppose that puzzle piece acts as a portal to take you somewhere else? Where would that place be?

Why pick me? Why choose you?

The idea germinated for a few days, and I wrote a story that became Pieces of Silver. The finished story ended up taking place in a puzzle store on the Florida panhandle with a central character who needed a reset in his life, even though he didn't realize it until the end.

Once I had Pieces of Silver completed, I wondered how Mac came to own the store, and began that story.

Something like two thousand words in, I realized it wasn't working. Only Travis McGee wins big things in card games, and I didn't like the person Mac was becoming. Mac wasn't the same man as in Pieces of Silver, and the story didn't quite fit the idea I had that he needed something resolved in his life.

I put that attempt in the "discard for now and look at later folder" and started again.

This time the story flowed a lot better. It came out much as I hoped, and The Tolling Bell tells how Mac comes to own The Puzzle Store.

These two stories bookend Tales from the Puzzle Store, and in between are three more never published stories that take you to England, California, and the Mediterranean.

And if you're ever driving along I-98 between Destin and

Santa Rosa Beach in Florida, keep an eye on the south side of the highway. Mac doesn't have a sign up, but you'll recognize the building, and he's always got coffee brewing.

You never know what you might find there.

THE TOLLING BELL

ONE

I'd played a solo round of golf as the sun came up, hitting the ball through the light mist and dew-soaked grass, and watching the resort slowly come to life. I grabbed a coffee from the urn in the pro-shop, then got in the car and drove west along I-98, leaving Miramar Beach behind and going with the flow until I got to the Alabama state line.

By that time the coffee was cold, and I'd driven eighty miles without being fully aware of my surroundings.

I'd done that a lot in the last three months. Living in a haze like the mist blurring the greens that morning. It will take time, the doctor had said, but he hadn't held his dead wife in his arms. I parked in the lot of a restaurant and sat watching the low slow rollers come up the Gulf and curl lazily onto the narrow strip of sand the restaurant advertised as a beach.

After I'd laid Beth to rest and dealt with all the legal and administrivia that goes with the death of a spouse, my life was empty and without purpose. I'd been fortunate enough to step away from regular day-to-day work four years ago, and now I wondered why. Not that I wanted to go back to it. The industry had changed and technology had moved beyond my desire to catch up.

A pair of gulls cruised the surf line, floating along on the breeze. They spotted something, folded their wings and dived, barely making a splash as they entered the water. I envied their purpose, even if it was just for food. On cue, my stomach growled, reminding me that cold coffee wasn't a good source of nutrition.

I didn't want to stop and eat so compromised with a chicken sandwich from a drive-thru and managed not to dribble mayo on my jeans.

I was midway between Destin and Miramar Beach when I saw the restaurant on the south side of I-98. The blue painted two-story building stood forlorn and alone in the middle of a sunken and otherwise empty lot with a parking area of crumbling concrete slabs that spun loose pieces stone into the underside of my Corvette with a discordant symphony of bangs and clangs that made me fear for the tailpipe or even worse, the transmission.

I braked, slowed to the equivalent of a slow walk, and coaxed the low chassis over the last fifty feet of rough ground, turning the wheel carefully to avoid several puddles of dirt brown water.

Close up, the eggshell blue paint was peeling from the walls, the guttering sagged in a couple of places, and there were rust-colored stains on the concrete where the runoff had pooled and dried in the hot Florida sunshine.

I uncurled myself from the driver's seat, stood with my hands on the roof of the car and twisted my back until I felt the lower vertebrae click back in to place. At fifty-nine, I was really too damn old to be driving a car you almost had to crawl in and out of, but I'd had this car twenty years and loved it as much as the day I bought it.

The windows were dusty and grimy and dulled the appearance of the lights inside. The silver aluminum door frame was pitted with white corrosion spots. I'd noted the cracks in the concrete roof tiles as I came off the highway and wondered if the red neon sign saying "Open" was telling the truth.

The handle was loose, and when I pulled the door open, there was a squeal of metal across concrete.

Inside, the air was cool, circulating slowly and keeping out the ever present Florida humidity. I was expecting tables and chairs and a bar, and more light from the few working fluorescent tubes above my head. There was more light coming through the dirty windows behind me than the lights provided. In front I saw a waist-high counter and shoulder high shelving stretching off to the right and all the way to the back wall. From the back of the store, I could hear the excited chatter of commentary on a ball game.

This wasn't a restaurant. It was a retail store of some kind.

"Hallo," I called and moved toward the counter.

"Be right with you," a voice hollered back. The noise of the ball game stopped, and I heard the scuff of feet come along one of the shelving aisles.

"Hi," he said. "I'm Josh. You looking for a jigsaw puzzle?"

He topped my six-one by a couple of inches. I guessed he was in his early twenties. He looked like he was still growing into his gangly body and the Crimson Tide sweat shirt hung loosely on his shoulders.

"I was looking for coffee. I assumed this was a restaurant."

Josh smiled, showing a set of even white teeth. "About ten years ago, it was. The restaurant went out of business and my grandfather bought it. He made it one of the top five puzzle stores in the country."

I glanced around and despite my best efforts, couldn't keep the surprise off my face.

"I know," he said with an apologetic smile. "You wouldn't think it today. Grandad died nearly a year ago, and the store stayed closed. My Dad and his brother decided it was time to do something with the place, so I agreed to come down, clean it up and open for business." He ran a hand through his tousled black hair. "I brought a machine with me so I can make coffee if you'd like. If you don't mind the dust, look around as well. It's no trouble and I'll be glad of the company."

"Thank you," I said. "Black's fine." If I was honest, I'd be glad of the company as well. Someone who didn't know me, who hadn't known Beth and would talk about normal things. "What puzzles would you recommend?"

He shrugged. "It's still new to me. Kids' puzzles are at the front on your right. The more complex puzzles go all the way back. We've got anything from cities to landscapes and fantasy. There's an entire section on Game of Thrones and Harry Potter."

He turned away to get the coffee started, and I drifted over to the children's puzzle area. There were wooden chairs, stools and tables all at the low height suitable for five or six-year-olds. A selection of puzzles was laid out on the tables, the artwork on the boxes faded and curling at the edges. With proper lighting, and without the dust, it would be a welcoming area.

I don't have grandchildren. Not yet anyway, so I carried on into the stacks of adult jigsaws. The sheer volume was amazing. There must have been hundreds of puzzles along the shelves. I didn't realize anyone under seventy-five still bought them.

I had old memories of visits to my grandmother in Rhode Island. Most times she had a piece of plywood laid over the lace tablecloth of her dining table. A board we had to move before eating, and move carefully so as not to disturb the partially completed puzzle on the board.

In Tampa or Palm Beach, I could see the attraction, but

Destin and Miramar Beach are known more for golf and spring break than retirement communities.

The nearest shelves had boxes with city views on the front, London, Rome, Paris, and cities I couldn't recognize without the text telling me it was Prague or Vancouver. Each puzzle was between two and five thousand pieces.

I couldn't imagine Grandma tackling one of these. A thousand or fifteen hundred pieces were her standard, and they could take her a week or more to complete. Who has the time, or desire, to put together three thousand pieces of card, all different shapes and colors?

As I walked down the aisle toward the back of the store, the pictures on the box tops changed from cities to landscape and nature. I wasn't really looking, skimming the surface really and killing time until the coffee arrived. Not that I had anywhere to go, or to be. That was the one thing I'd allowed retirement to take away from me: the soaking up of knowledge and instant decision making.

I reached the back wall where the light was dim. The box pictures here were bright neons and pastels and seemed to shine through the gloom. Except one where the picture was white and every shade of gray. The contrast made it stand out from the other jigsaws. I paused part way through turning as the image caught my eye.

The puzzle was an Escher: Ascending and Descending. One character, the one in the blue jacket, looked up. His gray eyes transfixed me.

TWO

The air was still, like it hadn't moved in hours or days, and I caught a faint tang of sweat and the odor of stale breath. The stone stairs under my feet were hard and unyielding. Each step sent aching stabs of pain up each leg and into my hips, Blue Jacket's hips, with every step Blue Jacket took. It was like I was Blue Jacket, or somehow I was in him.

I had no idea how I got here or, other than on Escher's Tower, where I really was. I hovered in a state between panic and disbelief. While I did so, we kept walking. Blue Jacket trudged with a steady and measured pace that kept him the same distance between the person ahead and the person behind. We reached a platform at the top of the stairs, turned right and continued climbing.

As we turned onto the second flight, I saw more of the surroundings. Down to the left was a sloping tiled roof with a chimney that and billowed puffs of gray smoke. Below the chimney there was a courtyard with a low retaining wall to prevent anyone falling two storeys to the ground.

All around me there was a soft hum like a chant or a

mantra, but it was too low and too indistinct for me to make out the words if there were any.

At the top of the steps ahead there was a brick structure with a sloping tiled roof and a weather vane that seemed stuck pointing away from the tower. Everything in a different shade of gray.

I'd first thought the only color was gray, but as we climbed the second flight, I became aware of the line of people on my right, all of them marching down the steps we were climbing.

Or were they marching up? Wasn't that the illusion of the Escher's? Down was up and up was down.

It surprised me to see the occasional color. More blue jackets, and as my eyes became accustomed to the dull gray light, I saw a more infrequent splash of pink as well.

We reached the top of this flight right in front of the brick structure, and underneath the weather vane, I felt Blue Jacket hesitate, his eyes sliding to the right. I glimpsed a pink jacket and a curl of blonde hair, then we were climbing again, the weather vane above me, and down to the right another gray staircase and beyond it the anonymity of the gray cloud that surrounded the tower, leaving it isolated and alone in whatever world we were in.

By my estimation, it took fifteen minutes to cover the next two flights, make a turn at the bell tower. There was a huge bell hanging from the cross struts, silvery-gray and looking like it hadn't been rung in a very long time.

This time I was paying attention and there was a definite hitch in his step when he caught sight of the blonde as she trudged her own path upward.

That was the only highlight. The climbing continued endlessly. Thirty minutes for a circuit. Then another, and another. No one stopped. No one flagged. No one ate, and the surrounding light never changed.

Mostly the people kept their heads down, hands in the

pockets of their jackets, and lifted one foot onto the next step, then the other. As we continued the procession, I noticed the blues and pinks fading into the dull uniform gray of this world. It started on the sleeves and crept up past the elbows to the collar.

I lost count of how many circuits we'd completed with the gray growing when I finally made sense of the humming murmur around me.

"Nowhere to be. Nothing to do. Nowhere to go."

A mantra chanted by everyone on the stairs, whichever direction they walked. The words definitely matched my mood, and I wondered if that had brought me to wherever this was.

More circuits, and I felt the restlessness growing in Blue Jacket every time we passed her. I couldn't tell if he knew the blonde woman or if he sensed a connection between them, but it disturbed him and I felt the frustration building inside him.

From then on, I attempted to keep count. Four circuits an hour. Forty circuits. Ten hours. Every circuit, I kept telling Blue Jacket to do something. I couldn't feel any difference in him, although it looked like the creeping gray had paused around the elbows of his jacket.

I still don't know if Blue Jacket did it. If I did it, or if it was a joint effort by both of us, but during the eleventh hour, as we reached the corner by the weather vane, his hand came out of his coat pocket. The fingers were pale and twisted like a claw. As we turned the corner, his arm stretched out across the gap, brushing against the pink sleeve of the blonde's jacket. Her head snapped up, fear and surprise clouding her china-blue eyes. We were almost past when I saw the hint of a smile curve her lips upward and her head lifted a few inches.

Two flights. Fifteen minutes. Maybe the longest fifteen

minutes in my life other than when I'd held Beth in my arms waiting for the paramedics to arrive.

Blue Jacket was changed. He still chanted the mantra, but there was new life and a note of defiance in his voice. His body thrummed with an energy that hadn't been there before, and I noticed the gray had retreated to the cuffs of the jacket sleeves.

At the Bell Tower corner, I felt the anticipation tremble through him. He stretched his hand out again. His fingers trembled a little.

This time she was prepared.

Her head came up, blue eyes alive as her own hand crossed the divide and touched his. The pale pink of her jacket blossomed into a rich rose color.

High above us the bell in the tower tolled a high clear note.

THREE

I leaned against the shelving and sucked in huge gasps of air like I hadn't breathed in hours. My head spun and the grinding ache in my legs and arms was like I'd run an ultra-marathon.

Not that I ever had, but it really felt like it. I walked slowly back to the front of the store, trying not to limp.

"Are you okay?" Josh asked when he saw me, a concerned frown on his narrow face as he offered the mug of coffee.

I nodded. I wasn't sure I was ready to trust myself to speak.

"You sure? You look awful pale," he dragged a metal folding chair from behind the counter, the legs scraping on the concrete floor. "Sit here for a moment. Did something happen to you?"

The chair was solid under my sore thighs, the cool of the metal through my jeans a reminder of the real world. The aroma of the coffee and its bitter taste another reminder.

"My wife died six months ago," I said. "Totally unexpected. She had a brain aneurysm and was gone before I realized she had a problem."

"I'm sorry," he sounded embarrassed, knowing as I did that any words were inadequate.

"The people who are supposed to know tell me what happened to Beth is easier in the long run. I never had the other option, so I can't tell if they're right."

"Between the cancer and the dementia, Grandad lingered for months. No one in the family admits it openly, but when he finally passed away, everyone breathed a huge sigh of relief." He looked down at his coffee, then at me like he was about to say something, but there was the screech of metal on concrete and the door opened.

A young couple came in. I didn't pay attention, and Josh got up to help them, leaving me to think about what had happened, try to make sense of it. Although if I was being honest, and thinking objectively, the message was pretty clear.

"You want another coffee?" Josh stood before me and pointed at the mug.

"Please," I handed him the empty mug.

The couple were at the door, their bag of purchases heavy in his right hand while his left rested in the small of her back just below the flowing swathe of blonde hair. As he stepped out behind her, he glanced back over the shoulder of his blue denim jacket, his look catching my attention. There was a challenge in his gray eyes.

I let the idea roll quickly around my head, playing the what-if games I used to put on white boards.

When Josh came back, I accepted the steaming coffee. "If we called your father and your uncle," I said. "Do you think they'd sell me the store?"

I didn't have anywhere to go, but I'd have plenty to do.

THE TURBULENT PRIEST

ONE

The highway had been clear all the way from I-10 south down to I-98. The lights stayed green and Erin had pushed the Mustang hard. She covered the twenty miles in just under fifteen minutes, with her eyes squinted against the late afternoon sun that burned into her face from just above the pines.

She gunned the engine again when she turned west on I-98, reveling in the throaty roar and letting the adrenaline rush bleed away some of the anger still burning inside her.

Ahead, the light turned yellow.

Erin thought about running it until she saw the police cruiser hunkered down on the median. The Mustang's rear end fishtailed a little when she trod on the brakes, but there was no squeal from the tires, and she pulled up just short of the line.

The cop looked over, gave her a hard stare.

Erin met his gaze with an apologetic smile and breathed deeply. She could imagine the headlines if she collected a ticket. Given her current mood, it would likely be much more than speeding.

Erin decided it was time to get off the road and restore

some calm. When the light turned green, she let the grandmother in the Lexus roar ahead, even though her instinct was to pile on the gas and accelerate away, burn off more of the anger.

Instead, she drove a half-mile, crossed to the south side of the highway and pulled into a dirt parking lot. Why this particular lot she had no idea, and the bouncing as she coasted the sports car slowly over the uneven gravel and cracked concrete did nothing to improve her mood.

She eased to a stop before a big square blue painted building. The paint was flaking in places and the building looked like it should be a restaurant rather than some form of retail. The sign in the window said they were open and offered fresh coffee, so Erin opened the car door and clambered out into the humid Florida afternoon.

Close up, Erin could see brown water stains on the fading blue paint where the guttering had overflowed onto the wall. The aluminum framed door caught on the threshold and squealed when she opened it, making her tense. Lord, she was wound tighter than a drum and as empty as the bowl her cat had licked clean that morning.

The man behind the counter looked up, adjusted the half-moon glasses on his lined, craggy face, and gave her a smile of welcome.

"Looking for anything specific, or just here to browse, Reverend?"

Erin had seriously considered removing the collar tab when she got into the car, but she'd earned it despite the seemingly never-ending barbs directed at her from the Church Committee. Now, she wished she'd removed the tab.

Just wearing it reminded her of the fighting. Of the Committee wanting to spend six figures to replace the church organ when there were families in the community unable to clothe and feed themselves.

"If I'm honest, it was the coffee that called to me," she said with a smile. She let her gaze take in the comfortable seating area on her left and the children's space to the right. Behind the counter and stretching away beyond the children's space were rows of shoulder high shelving stacked with jigsaw puzzles. The entire space felt bright, airy, and welcoming. Pine scent drifted to her from the candles she could see burning on the low coffee table in the comfortable space.

Erin loved the smell of pine, its heady scent doing more to relax and ground her than the crazed drive south from Dothan. She realized the man behind the counter was saying something.

"If you don't mind waiting a few minutes, I'll brew a fresh pot," he said. "This one's been getting stale and burned for nearly an hour."

"I can wait," Erin said and turned away as her phone buzzed. When she looked at the display, there was a text from her friend Rhonda. She grimaced at the panicked tone of the words and pushed the phone back into her pocket. She needed to consider her words carefully before replying.

"Is it okay if I look round?"

"Please do," the man said. "Hopefully you'll buy at least one of our puzzles. I'm Mac, shout for me if you have questions."

Erin really wanted to sink into the love seats to her left, feel the cushions curl around her and let the warm sun ease the chill and ache in her bones. She'd been fighting for so long, she was worn down and while the anger fueled her adrenaline and passion. It still didn't fill the empty hole inside her that had once been belief.

She skirted the low wooden tables and chairs in the children's space, stepped over brightly colored pieces of puzzles scattered over the floor, and entered an aisle labeled Cities and Towns. There were a few American cities featured, but the majority were in Europe. Paris, Rome, Madrid. All the places she'd wanted to visit and put the plans aside when she entered seminary.

It was a decision she couldn't change, even if now she wasn't sure it was the right one.

At the end of the aisle, Erin was at the back of the store. The bright glare of the sun didn't reach this far back. Despite the overhead glare of the fluorescent lighting, it felt dimmer, and there was a slight chill in the air that made her tuck her hands under her arms.

Erin started to walk back down the same aisle, decided she didn't need to indulge her pity-party by looking at more cities she'd never visit. She stepped across to the next aisle.

There were no labels here, and after a couple of paces, she recognized the theme. Paintings. Mainly Old Masters: Caravaggio and Da Vinci. Personally, she preferred the softer colors and muted hues of Monet, Degas, and Renoir, and there were some of those as well. As the images transitioned from classic to modern, a darker image on the bottom shelf caught her attention.

Erin squatted down on her haunches, brushing a strand of hair off her face as she reached for the puzzle box, and read the title: The Martyrdom of Thomas-a-Becket by Thomas Stothard. She didn't recognize the artist, but she'd studied the many early martyrs during seminary.

As her fingers tilted the box, Thomas ducked away from the four Knights surrounding him. His dark brown eyes locked with Erin's.

TWO

If the back of the store had been cool, Erin was now chilled. Bitter air nipped at her nose and ears, seared the back of her throat. Her breath clouded in the air as she moved between the tall stone pillars of the Cloister.

Except it wasn't her breath and the voice murmuring the Gloria was deeper and more masculine than her voice ever would be. His heavy wool cloak provided minimal protection from the icy wind that flowed over the high stone walls and swirled around the wide open space of the cloister driving eddies of snow into her face, the flakes gray in the sputtering light of the torches set under the portico.

This is a dream, Erin told herself. I stood up too quickly, got dizzy and passed out. I am not in the body of Thomas-a-Becket about to face his murderers. She wondered if you could acknowledge dreaming while in a dream.

Or was God testing her?

Erin had preached sermons on signs and wonders and how they still mattered in the twenty-first century. Had the emptiness in her soul hardened her to the point where she could no longer accept miracles?

The crunch of feet on the icy ground on the far side of the Cloister made Thomas pause. He peered forward as four shapes billowed out of the darkness. Erin thought of wraiths and wanted to squeal, but Becket seemed calm, almost relaxed.

"Welcome my Lords," he said. "What brings you to Canterbury on this dark night?"

The men came to a halt before him, three spaced in a wide arc and the fourth a pace or two ahead, close enough that Erin could smell the fetid warmth of his breath.

"You must come to Winchester with us, Priest. King Henry demands an accounting of your actions this past November."

"Then I fear your journey has been in vain," Becket replied in a firm voice that gave Erin insight into how this son of a textile merchant had become Archbishop of Canterbury. Becket straightened, the robe's ermine hood falling back, and despite the sudden wave of cold air, Erin felt the man's power.

"I answer to the Lord and to His Holiness, Pope Alexander," Thomas said. "If the King cannot respect the role of this Cathedral during coronations, the Church cannot support him as a member."

"Those are treasonous words, Priest."

Becket turned to face the Knight who'd spoken of treason. The man was on the far left of the three, and the nearby torch highlighted his dark hair and beard crusted with ice and snow. Anger glittered in his dark eyes. His hand was at his waist where a sword would normally rest. Morville or Fitz-Urse, Erin guessed, interpreting Becket's thoughts, although no worthwhile images of these men had survived the centuries.

"It is a long journey to Winchester," Thomas said in a mild tone. "You are welcome to eat with us after Vespers and stay the night."

"This is not over," the leader, Richard le Breton, growled. He turned on his heel and with a wave of his arm, led his companions back the way they'd come.

Becket spoke without turning his head. "You can come out of the shadows, Grim. They're gone for the moment."

The secretary revealed himself with a series of small steps that brought him into the flickering light of the torch. He was shorter and more rotund than Becket. His face was red and pinched with the cold.

"You sound sure they'll return, Your Grace."

"With the anger they carry inside, a simple refusal will not deter them, Grim," he turned and extended his arm. "Come, let us not keep Prior Robert and our Brothers waiting to celebrate Vespers."

As they walked along the Cloister toward the Chapter House, Erin didn't know what to think. This man had excommunicated his King and stood against four Knights with no more fear than she felt when crossing a busy street. She had stood against her church elders over an organ and felt like the hounds of hell had been unleashed on her. What must it be like for him?

She missed the question Grim asked, but Becket's answer stunned her.

"The excommunication wasn't something I did in a fit of pique, Grim. I spent many hours praying for other options and asking for guidance. When a King believes he is above God, nothing good comes from it. The fall of Judah shows us the end of that path."

The last bell calling the monks to prayer tolled as they entered the Chapter House, and Grim moved to the doors, gesturing at his fellow monks for help to drag the doors closed.

"What are you doing?"

"We must stop them if they return."

Fear pitched Grim's voice an octave higher as he pushed at the heavy oak door.

"No!"

It was the first time Erin heard Becket raise his voice, and it carried an authority and command that made the monks pause. They looked at him uncertainly.

"It is not right to make a fortress out of a house of prayer," he said. "If they return, I trust the Knights will respect the sanctity of this Cathedral. In the meantime, it is time for Vespers. You may close the doors against the cold Grim, but they are not to be bolted or secured shut."

Prior Robert, a tall thin ascetic man with barely enough hair to form a tonsure, officiated the Vespers service. Erin felt Becket struggle with his understanding of the Latin verses and the expected responses.

The Vespers Psalm was read, the Gloria being chanted when the doors crashed open. Richard le Breton and his three companions pushed their way inside, bringing a blast of chill air with them. The chant faltered. Robert's eyes flicked questioningly to Becket, who shook his head and waved for the Prior to continue.

As Robert began the Lord's Prayer, Becket moved to the side, hastening away from the other monks toward the room that connected the Chapter House to the nave of the Cathedral.

Becket was not a man of action, his breathing was heavy and labored as he hurried from the Chapter House, Grim and the Knights close behind. Erin could feel his thoughts like her own, or was it a prayer as he echoed the words of Jesus in a low murmur no-one else would hear. "Father, if it is possible, let this cup pass from me."

He knows, Erin realized. He knows what will happen.

The four soldiers crammed into the room behind them, forcing Becket back against the far wall and giving him no access to the stairs leading down to the crypt, or up to the quire.

"I am no traitor," Becket said as de Tracy stepped forward, twisted his arm into Becket's robe, dragged him toward the cloister door.

There was a scuffle behind Erin, an angry growl from one of the Knights and a wail of pain from Grim.

Erin wanted to lash out and scream, fight back in any way she could to support Grim. Becket wrapped his arms round one of the stone pillars, the cold of the stone burned though his clothes as gripped hard to resist de Tracy's attempt to drag him away.

Erin heard a swish through the air as Becket bowed his head.

It was like cracking her head into a concrete wall. Numbness at first, then a searing blinding pain. Despite his mental desire to be stoic, Thomas cried out, then again as another sword cleaved into his skull.

Stay down, Erin cried at him through the pain. Keep low and avoid the blows. You can get away from this and come back.

Becket couldn't hear her. She felt his forehead rest against the cold stone of the pillar, felt the sting of blood in his eyes as it dripped from the wounds in his scalp onto the black velvet of his robe, felt the calm in his body as he ignored her pleas, drew breath and lifted his head as the third blow struck.

THREE

Erin sobbed a breath in, let it out, and gulped in more. The jigsaw puzzle was still in her hands and she'd dropped forward onto her knees.

Carefully, forcing her shaking hand to be still, she replaced the puzzle onto the wooden shelf and ran her hand over her scalp, feeling for the wounds she knew must be there.

Nothing. No wound and no blood.

Just the silky feel of short black hair under her fingers. Another breath, and Erin used the support from the shelves to stand.

The light at the front of the store seemed incredibly bright, and she half closed her eyes as she walked down the aisle to the children's section and turned toward the counter.

"Just in time," Mac said, handing her a mug with steam rising in a soft gray cloud that reminded her of their breaths in the Cloister.

"You have an interesting store, Mr. Mac."

"Just Mac. I still think anyone calling me Mister is referring to my father, and he died when I was in my twenties."

"It's still an interesting store," she said. She lowered herself onto the love seat facing away from the window and sipped at the coffee Mac had given her.

She waited until he slid onto the seat opposite, then continued.

"Did you know something would happen?"

"Specifically, no. In the time I've owned the store, I sometimes get a feeling someone may have an experience."

"Has it happened to you?"

He nodded. "The experience can be enlightening."

Erin waited, but clearly he wasn't going to say anything more.

"What do you mean by enlightening?"

"Not everyone talks to me about it," he said. "Those who do have a common theme. They come away with a better understanding of their lives. It's not always a step forward. Sometimes it's a step sideways, or even back."

"I must have missed something," Erin said, struggling to keep the frustration out of her voice. Sure, the anger inside had subsided, but she knew there was something more. Something deeper, but she just couldn't see it.

Mac leaned forward, the light streaming in from the windows behind her flashing on his half-moon glasses. His voice was low, deep, and encouraging. "Think about what you saw and heard. Don't analyze it, just walk it through in your mind."

"Easy for you to say."

Erin frowned at him, sipped her coffee and sat forward, hunching her shoulders almost to her ears. She felt the heat of the sun on her neck, the scent of the pine candles relaxing her as she thought through everything that happened after she picked up the puzzle box.

"He prayed."

It came out in a soft breath. Then louder. "Becket prayed

for any option other than excommunication until he had no choice. I don't pray."

Mac raised an eyebrow.

"Well, I do. In services, and as part of my daily devotional, but not as a way to solve a problem, or seek guidance. I used to."

When did I stop, Erin asked herself, although in her heart she already knew the answer. It was around the time she started believing only she knew the right way forward.

Erin lifted the mug, saw it was still two-thirds full, and put it back on the coaster. Dothan was a good two-hour drive away.

"I have to go," she said.

Mac stood as she did, and impulsively she leaned over the narrow table and hugged him. When she pulled back, his craggy face was flushed and there was a smile on his face.

Erin pulled slowly out of the parking lot, careful not to spin gravel or debris that might chip the Mustang's pristine red paintwork.

She used hands free to call Rhonda as the light ahead went red.

"No questions," she ordered when her friend answered. "Get the Committee together. I want everyone in the church in three hours."

"To what purpose?" Rhonda had been right beside her through all the trials.

"We're going to pray," Erin said as the light turned green.

She couldn't help herself. The cop was gone from the median, so she pushed her right foot to the floor and accelerated away from the grandmother in the Lexus.

THE PIRATE PUZZLE

ONE

Tripp drummed his fingers on the steering wheel of the rented SUV. Tourists clustered around the pools in the condo complexes on his left. The sun bounced off the sparkling blue waters of the Gulf on his right, making the wrap around aviator sunglasses essential protection from the glare.

Ahead of him the road was empty, and he itched to drive his right foot to the floor and unleash the engine's power. The speed bumps every two hundred yards made him pause, and the Sheriff's cruiser hugging his rear fender was a more powerful deterrent.

But he really wanted to let loose, use the speed as his first celebration of the acquisition he'd just closed. An acquisition that would turn a tired and dated amusement park into a modern and luxurious condo complex with security gates and private beach access for the wealthy owners. He could already see the finished development in his mind, and it felt good. Better than good, despite the attitude of the selling family. Tripp wasn't good with fancy words, but when the elderly patriarch called him rapacious, he suspected it wasn't a compliment.

Tripp decided it would be easier to cut through one of the side roads back onto I-98 and head east to Miramar Beach and back to the hotel. He could crack the first bottle of Moet there and save his need for speed until he got onto I-10 in the morning.

The traffic on I-98 crawled and as he looked at the passing buildings, Tripp initially thought the half-acre lot next to the highway was empty, a huge expanse of brown sandy soil and tufts or straggling grass coated with the dust blown by the continual streams of traffic. On this stretch, Tripp guessed the zoning would be commercial. It didn't concern him. Tripp had the contacts to change that, even with the complication of the single building he could now see as the traffic inched forward.

The blue painted two story building looked like a restaurant. A struggling restaurant, Tripp thought as the excitement lifted his pulse. Almost without conscious thought, he was turning off the road toward the building, noting the cracks on the edges of the gray concrete roof tiles.

Tripp couldn't help smiling at the prospect of water damage on that second floor. It would help reduce the price, even though he'd rip the building down as soon as the papers were signed. This was an ideal position for a low to mid-range motel or an apartment block.

He was almost salivating when he reached the front of the store. The bottom of the door scraped on the concrete threshold with a squeal that made Tripp wince. Ahead of him was a counter with a computer monitor and a stack of glossy magazines. On the left was an open area with well-cushioned chairs, love seats and low tables.

Fluorescent lights in the ceiling cast an even, slightly yellow light over the shoulder high shelving that stretched away behind the counter and off to the right-hand side.

The inside was bigger than Tripp expected. There was a

tremendous amount of space if you ripped out the shelving units and so many possibilities. Perhaps it could be a clubhouse if he rethought the rest of the land and zoned it for an RV Park.

"Can I help you?"

The rich gravely voice cut into Tripp's thoughts, and when he looked up, there was a man there, leaning his elbows on the stone countertop. Tripp guessed the man was in his late fifties, hair receding from his forehead and turning silvery-gray. He looked to be a couple of inches taller than Tripp's six-feet, with wide shoulders and a hard body that looked like he was used to physical labor.

"I'm in real estate," Tripp said. "I was just passing and saw the property. Would you be interested in selling? I could offer you a good price."

Something flashed in the man's hazel eyes. "I'm sure you can," he said with a knowing smile.

Tripp watched as the man's expression turned thoughtful and his head tipped slightly to the left.

"I acquired this place a couple of years ago. On average, I get two or three offers a month. I appreciate the thought, but it's not for sale."

"You haven't heard my offer."

"I don't need to," he said with the same smile that was beginning to annoy Tripp. It was a smile that suggested the man was playing with him.

Tripp didn't like being played.

"I'm Mac," the man said. "I'll have coffee ready in a few minutes. Stay and have a mug with me and I'll tell you why I'm not interested in selling."

Mac said and gestured toward the racks of shoulder high shelving. "Have a look round while we're waiting, and maybe you'll see something you like."

I already see something I like and want, Tripp thought.

He said nothing, though. He'd made the first move and now it was up to the old man to make a counteroffer. He didn't believe there were two or three offers a month. Everyone had their price, and it was his job to find it. Having coffee with the man would give him more information, help him find that price.

Tripp ignored the open space to his left. He didn't want to sit in the comfortably upholstered chairs and have a meaningless conversation. He wanted to move around and browsing the shelves would keep him occupied until the coffee was ready. He was regretting making the stop and coming in here.

He shook his head as he weaved through the untidy cluster of children's chairs and low tables to the adult puzzles arranged on shoulder high shelves running all the way to the back of the store. It was pleasant in a family sort of way. His sister would love it, but Tripp knew families weren't for him. They got in the way.

The first aisle was all city scapes, and he mentally ticked off the US cities he'd visited and frowned at two pictures until he realized the cities were in flyover states, areas of the country where he had no desire to spend time.

Along the next aisle he saw rows of landscapes and seascape puzzles. Some seascapes were storms crashing against cliffs or around lighthouses. Others were of ships in battle and the title on one box made Tripp pause.

The picture on the box titled *End of the Soderina* was a pirate fleet bearing down on a fleeing merchant vessel. The detail in the picture was surprisingly clear, and despite himself, Tripp leaned forward, intrigued by the stance of the man standing on the raised aft deck of the pirate ship. The pirate captain raised his head and looked at Tripp.

TWO

Tripp's first thought was he was going to throw up. All his life, the pitching and swaying motion of any boat churned his stomach. He couldn't handle the big cruise ships that left from Port Lauderdale, and this one was nowhere near their size.

He was on the raised aft deck, and around him the ship made ship noises. The sails cracked as the wind rose and fell, the wooden railing before him creaked and there was the noise of the crew as they murmured in anticipation of what was to come.

On either side of the ship, two sloops kept station, their gun ports open and cannon run out ready for battle.

"Hold her steady," Tripp said to the helmsman beside him.

Except Tripp hadn't spoken, and he didn't have an English accent. The realization he was part of the Captain was frightening enough for him to forget the seasickness.

"Holding steady, Captain," the helmsman replied. "Are you sure they're carrying gold?"

"If not, they're all going to the bottom of the sea," the Captain said.

Tripp could feel the man's anticipation and excitement as he jammed his hands into the deep pockets of the heavy leather coat and paced the width of the quarterdeck. The coat provided warmth and protection from the chill autumn wind blowing out of the Eastern Mediterranean.

The captain, his name was Ward, had captured the *Soderina* six months ago and put her through an extensive refit in Tunis. The refit included reconfiguring the gun deck and installing four thirty-six pound long guns salvaged from the wreck of a French warship. He was eager to use those big guns for the first time.

A man clattered up the companionway from the main deck, the sword strapped to his waist jingling as he moved. He was about Tripp's height, nearly six feet, with long black hair tied back into a ponytail and a raw bony face with an ugly scar showing ivory on the brown skin of his face.

"Boarding party's ready, Captain Ward. They're eager for some action."

"I'm expecting they'll just have cleaning up to do. Our new cannon will win the day for us."

"I hope so. Some of the men are nervous about those cannon. They say they're too much for a ship like the *Soderina*."

"No cannon is too much, Yusuf," Ward crossed the deck, put his hand on the other man's shoulder, and turned him so they could both see the fleeing vessel. "Look at her, Yusuf. She sails as elegantly as my bathtub in Tunis. Men like that don't want to fight."

Tripp could feel the impatience inside the man. It was the same feeling Tripp had when someone dragged their feet on a property deal. The feeling that pushed him to do something he probably shouldn't.

Ward turned back to the helmsman. "Can you sail another

twenty degrees to port without needing to tack? I want to bring the guns to bear."

The man tilted his head back and studied the layers of patched ivory colored canvas stretching high above his head.

He frowned, poked his tongue into his cheek, making it bulge. Shook his head, then shrugged. "The winds all over the place. I can give you ten, probably fifteen degrees, but if the wind shifts too much we'll be in irons."

"I'll take that chance," Ward said, then to Yusuf. "Tell the gunner to fire as he bears on the target. And remind him to aim for the masts. If he sinks that ship, I'll take the lost prize money out of his hide."

Yusuf grinned, his scar becoming more prominent. "You tell him that every time, but I'll remind him. And I'll remind you he hasn't let us down yet."

Looking toward the bow, Tripp watched the outline of the other vessel move from left to right. Around him the sails spilled air and began a lazy flapping that to Tripp sounded like a leather belt being slapped across a table. The hull groaned. Tripp watched water squeeze out of a rope thick as his wrist as the wind gusted and the sails cracked taut, giving *Soderina* momentum and moving her forward again, letting the helmsman swing the ship another few degrees to port.

Voices drifted up through the open hatches from the gun deck below. The voices fell silent and then there was a booming crash, followed by another. Smoke billowed up through the hatches, thick and gray and stinking of gunpowder. Tripp felt Ward's eyes water as the smoke flowed past them and then away as the wind caught it.

The boarding party on the main deck cheered as one of the shots hit the top of the target's foremast, sending it tumbling in a tangle of ropes, spars and sails.

In response, a pair of smaller cannon mushroomed smoke from their muzzles, the shot splashing down well short of the

Soderina at the same time the noise reached them. The calls of the boarding party became louder, and they waved pikes and cutlasses in the air.

The thirty-six pounders crashed again. More smoke poured up from below decks, with it the grinding sound of timbers collapsing and men screaming.

There was another double crash from below, but no more smoke. Tripp felt the unease ripple through Ward's body. No-one could reload a cannon that fast. The captain rushed toward the rail as men poured up from below decks.

"Water," they cried in four languages as they scrambled away from the lower decks. "We're taking on water."

"Impossible," Ward shouted at them. "Go back to your guns. We have a prize to capture."

Some of the men hesitated, half turning back to the hatches, and as they did so another booming crash assaulted their ears.

Soderina lurched to the left. Ward grabbed the railing to stop himself falling into the helmsman. High above them the mastheads whipped to the left, and two men lost their grip on the ratlines, their screams thin and high as they plunged into the cold Mediterranean waters.

"The cannons collapsed the gun deck," Yusuf said from the top of the companionway. At least one of them has holed the hull. I've got men on the pumps, but they can't keep pace.

"Then get more men down there," Ward snapped, then to the helmsman. "Get her back on course."

Soderina responded sluggishly and reluctantly. The sails filled and became taut, but there was none of the speed Tripp had felt earlier. Their quarry had cleared the tangle on lines and debris from the topgallants and was widening the gap between them.

Ward growled with anger and frustration. Tripp felt his

own fear merge with the pirate's. This was why he didn't spend time on boats of any size.

"Heave to," Yusuf yelled from the hatch leading to the gun deck. "You must heave to. You're making the water flood faster. Another gun's on the edge."

The ship lurched again, settling a little deeper into the water, the recent burst of speed draining away as the bow tipped forward. There was a rending, splintering crash from below and the many screams of pain and terror.

The other cannon.

Tripp knew it at the same time the realization hit Ward. The pirate's fear blossomed into near terror.

"Signal our other ships," Ward ordered the helmsman. "Have them rescue anyone in the water and swing out our boats."

He flung the last over his shoulder as he hurried down the companionway onto the main deck, then through a pair of doors into the aft section of the ship. The bow tilted down further as Ward hurried along the dark, damp passageway, through another door and into the spacious aft cabin.

By this time he was walking on an upward incline, keeping his balance by holding onto the bulkheads. Bright light flooded through the stern windows, illuminating the glass-fronted cabinets and the oak dining table that dominated the width of the cabin. Ward skirted round the table and crossed to a wooden chest under the windows. He flung it open, and Tripp knew if he'd been himself, his mouth would have dropped open.

Ward reached in and pushed through the layers of fine silk and damask clothing to a leather bag. Tripp felt his arm muscles bunch and strain as Ward lifted the bag out of the chest, the contents chinking and jingling as he pushed it into his coat pocket.

The ship pitched forward again, the angle on the deck

became steeper. Ward shifted a step to keep his balance. From beyond the door there was the crash of furniture, the noise of shattering glassware and the frightened shouts of the crew.

Ward pushed through a door out onto a small balcony that hung off the stern of the ship. He stepped over a coil of rope and leaned over the waist-high rail. Tripp felt himself go dizzy at the long drop to the water below. He felt Ward about to pull back when a shout made him stop and look again.

There was a longboat below them, coming round the stern of the *Soderina*.

The sailor standing in the stern waved and shouted again. "Down here. We'll pick you up."

Ward bent down and lifted the rope coil. He tied one end to the railing and tossed the coil over the edge, then followed it.

Ward was subdued and spent the week of the return journey in the aft cabin he'd commandeered from the sloop's captain. For Tripp, it was seven days of torture. The weather changed on the second day, and the sloop pitched, rolled and yawed through a seemingly never-ending storm all the way to Tunis.

During his bouts of nausea, Tripp listened as the officers on the sloop brought news of the *Soderina*'s survivors. There were four others on this sloop, seven on the other. Eleven men from three hundred.

Yusuf wasn't among them.

The watchtowers at Ben Arous sighted them early on the morning of the eighth day. By the time the sloop entered Tunis Harbor, Ward was dressed in his heavy sea coat again, the bag heavy in the pocket. He joined the other officers on the sloop's quarterdeck, and Tripp could feel the tension among the men as the anchor splashed into the water and the chain rattled after it.

"I'll have a boat take you ashore, Captain. I'm sure you'll want to report what happened with the *Soderina* to the Pasha, or Uthman Dey. I'll have armed sailors escort you."

"Thank you, Captain," Ward replied formally. Tripp could feel the man's mind pulling itself out of the torpor of the last days, scheming, planning and preparing. The fault would lie somewhere, anywhere but with him. If Yusuf truly had failed to survive, who better?

The wharf was crowded with people and as the longboat drew closer, Tripp could see they were mostly women with a common look about them. A look that reminded Tripp of staff at three hotels he'd acquired north of Orlando a few years ago. Their hopes and expectations turning to fear and anger when they learned they had no future.

Two sailors led them up the stone steps, with two behind Ward who trod carefully on the slippery, seaweed covered stone. As they reached the top of the steps, the crowd surged forward, crying questions and screaming for answers.

A woman stepped forward. She was dressed in a dress of rich green fabric that closely hugged her upper body and highlighted her rich brown skin. "Where is he, Ward?" she demanded. "Where's my husband?"

Ward glanced around for his escort, couldn't see them, and Tripp felt the nervousness in his stomach clench into genuine pain, and the fear follow it. "I don't know, Adeela. Yusuf and I got separated. I asked if the other sloop, the *Khalida,* picked him up, but no-one seems to know."

"You don't care," Adeela screamed at him. "You never have, Ward. You seduced Yusuf and the others with promises of gold and jewels and plunder and use it to outfit more ships. For what? How many ships do you need? How many lives will you sacrifice to build a navy that has no purpose?"

Ward stepped forward, his mouth opening to speak, but she slashed her hand before her, forcing him into silence.

"There's nothing you can say. The French or the British, or maybe even Uthman Dey, will come for you. Then you'll orphan more of our children and widow more of our women. You're a rapacious murderer," she finished and spat a gob of phlegm onto Ward's black leather shoes as she turned away.

Ward waved his hand to ward her away, and Tripp became aware the guard of sailors had disappeared. As the Yusuf's wife turned away himself, Ward dropped his guard for a moment, and it was all she needed.

Tripp sensed Adeela turn back. He tried to make Ward pay attention, but he couldn't, and then it was too late.

She rushed forward, her arm swinging, brushing past the arm Ward raised ineffectually at the last moment. The shard of jagged glass sliced through the white silk shirt and gouged a bloody ragged gash deep into Ward's forearm.

The pirate screamed as the blood spurted from his arm in a scarlet stream. Worse than the Orlando crowd, Tripp thought. He stumbled back, his head slamming against the stone pillar. Everything went blank.

THREE

Tripp stumbled back, knocking the puzzle off the shelf. It slapped into the floor and for a moment the sharp noise drowned out the wailing sound that surrounded him as he slumped to his knees, shivering and shaking.

He remained there on his knees, arms wrapped around his body until he realized the sobbing noise he could hear came from himself. Tripp forced himself to take a series of deep breaths, and as he gained the confidence, he had himself under control; he heard footsteps.

The old man was beside him, his hands on Tripp's shoulders, lifting him with a strength Tripp hadn't expected, and guiding him slowly and carefully back through the store to the comfortable chairs.

"Stay there," the old man said.

When he came back, Tripp had remembered the man's name, Mac pushed a mug of coffee into Tripp's still quivering fingers. Usually Tripp preferred cream and sugar, but this once he let the aroma float up into his nostrils. He inhaled, let out a sigh and looked up.

Mac sat on the love seat opposite, fingers curled around

his own mug, a look of concern in his hazel eyes and on his lined face.

"I've not seen it affect anyone like that before," he said.

"Before?"

"Some people come into the store and trigger an experience that's very personal to them. It can be very unsettling."

"Not the word I would use," Tripp said, taking a mouthful of coffee and nearly burning his tongue.

"Frightening might be better," Mac agreed. "It happened to me the first day I came in her. It's how I ended up buying the store. And why I won't sell."

"Earlier today," he stopped as something occurred to him. "Is it still Tuesday?"

Mac nodded.

"Earlier today, a man called me rapacious. I didn't know what he meant until the woman used the same word to the pirate. You know what I mean?"

"I don't," Mac said. "What happened to me is very different from the experience other people have. From the experience you had. My belief is whatever happens inside the puzzle teaches something, or points us in a new direction. Whether we listen is up to us."

Tripp thought about the words Mac had used. The parallels between Ward on the *Soderina*, and how he did business himself. He jumped and nearly splashed the dregs of coffee over himself when Mac touched his shoulder and offered the coffee carafe to him.

Tripp nodded thanks and held out his mug.

"I've always thought of myself as focused and dedicated, never rapacious. Never as a pirate. I don't like the idea of people thinking that way about me."

"Looking honestly at ourselves in the mirror can be the hardest thing we do," Mac said.

"I know that now."

Tripp reached into a pocket for his phone.

"Would you excuse me for a moment?"

He walked over to the window, waiting for the person at the other end to answer.

Tripp took a deep breath when the connection was made.

"Mr. Hill, I've been thinking about our contract. I believe we can do better for your employees and your family. I could be there in about twenty minutes if you're prepared to talk."

He listened for a moment, then watched his reflection break into a smile. "No, Mr. Hill, I haven't been drinking, and I promise I won't get a ticket on the way. Thank you."

A WOMAN WHO DARED

ONE

Megan shivered and pulled the light shell jacket tighter around her shoulders as a wind gust whipped the rain into a brief maelstrom that finished the job of soaking her from head to toe.

She cursed, then again as a fast-moving SUV plowed through a pool of standing water, generating a small tidal wave that flung muddy water over her legs and drenched her sneakers.

Megan sighed and shifted the bag on her shoulder, put her head down and focused on putting one squelchy foot in front of the other. She swore to herself she wouldn't cry but cleaning the mess in a rent by the hour motel for less than minimum wage and carrying everything she valued in the bag on her shoulder was overwhelming.

There was nowhere safe in the single wide she shared with two other women, and she was sure Zoe was turning tricks to fund a habit. She'd walked in on Zoe two days ago and found her on her knees with her head buried in a man's crotch. Megan was sure she didn't want to live through that visual again.

Despite her vow, Megan felt the tears roll down her damp cheeks as another car sprayed her legs with more scummy road water.

On her right-hand side, the bushes and scrub died away and Megan saw an open expanse of dirt and gravel with a two-story building in the middle of the lot. The walls were painted a powder blue color, and the gray concrete roof tiles looked cracked in few places.

On a regular day, she'd have trudged past, just like she'd done for the hundred or so other days since she'd been making the journey back and forth.

Today Megan was bone-tired and she really, really didn't want to go back to that single-wide.

Not yet anyway.

There was a concrete walkway round the building and enough of an overhang she could shelter from the rain for a while, maybe warm up enough to stop shivering. Without giving herself time to think, and decide it was a bad idea, Megan splashed across the parking lot, the damp sand and gravel leaving more dirty smears across her calves and shins.

The wall was hard and gritty against her back, and the overhang didn't give her the protection she'd hoped for. Rain dripped from the guttering above and whipped into her face, and Megan wanted nothing more than to curl up somewhere, sob out the frustration and eviscerate Cole in her mind.

Despite the evidence, Cole had denied the embezzlement all the way to sentencing. With their joint assets confiscated, he was two years into a fifteen to twenty sentence in the Federal prison at Coleman. He remained oblivious to the devastation he'd caused in Megan's life. Oblivious that his actions had her disqualified as a CPA and the only work she could get was low wage.

There was a squealing, scraping noise as the door of the store opened. Megan pushed away from the wall, ready for the angry words and preparing to splash her way back across the muddy ground to the highway.

"Why don't you come inside where it's dry. I've got coffee brewing and you look like you could use a warm drink."

Megan lifted her head and looked, tensing her body for the payoff of some cruel joke.

The man standing in the doorway was nearly a foot taller than her five-two. Wide shoulders, thinning brown hair, and a gentle smile on his lined face. His smile faded as he sensed her reluctance.

"I mean it. Florida rain isn't always like warm bath water. You'll catch the flu or something worse in this weather."

He looked harmless, so Megan took a chance. Something she hadn't done in the past three years.

"Thank you," she said, and almost moaned as the warmth of the inside washed over her.

"They call me Mac," he said, pulling the door closed behind them. The frame squealed again, making Megan jump.

"I've been meaning to fix that since the day I bought the store," Mac apologized. "But it's cheaper than a bell if I'm in the back of the store and someone comes in. There's a place to sit on your left. You take milk or sugar."

"Just black," she said, heading in the direction he indicated. She hadn't been able to afford sugar or creamer for so long, she doubted she'd ever go back to them.

The area was laid out like a cozy sitting room. There were two love seats and a low table by the window, three more love seats with beige cushions and a dark wood table covered the center of the area. Two candles burned in squat jars on the table, adding a pleasant piney scent to the room.

Along the wall there were racks of shelves with boxes of jigsaw puzzles. She hadn't expected jigsaws. It reminded her of the summers before she was a teenager with visits to her aunt and half-finished puzzles in the dining room.

"Sit down," Mac said, walking past her. He placed two steaming mugs on coasters and pointed at the love seat opposite where he'd seated himself with a weary sigh. "I'm glad for the break. I know those orders won't fill themselves. Don't worry about the cushions. They're meant for outdoor furniture and are ideal when I have four-year-olds running around the place."

"Four-year-olds can be a handful," Megan said carefully as she sat and reached for the coffee. Her sister's boys had been that age when the charges were filed. As she sipped the hot drink, feeling the warmth flood through her, Megan wondered if she'd ever see them again.

They sat in a companionable silence. Megan was grateful Mac didn't ask questions or push her into conversation. She could see how tired he was from the dark shadows round his eyes, and the way his head drooped occasionally.

"I'm sorry to be a nuisance, but is there a bathroom I could use?"

"Hardly a nuisance. I invited you in on a slow customer day. Behind the counter and all the way to the back by the stairs. Mind the piles of packages for shipping," he said, then pointed to the bag she'd instinctively hoisted onto her shoulder when she stood. "You can leave your bag here. I promise it will be safe."

Megan nodded. She wanted to trust him, but the few items of any value she owned were in that bag. Most of it was emotional rather than monetary value. The thought of losing anything more was almost too much to bear.

"I'll take it with me, if you don't mind."

"Whatever you're comfortable with," Mac said.

She saw the understanding in his hazel eyes, and that made her feel a little better.

As Megan threaded her way through the stacks of shipping boxes in the hallway, she wondered where and how Mac had gained that insight and understanding.

Coming out of the bathroom. Megan felt better than she had in a long time, probably since she'd started the job at the motel. She'd cleaned the mud streaks off her legs and oddly, she felt comfortable here, and although her clothes were still damp, for once she was warm. Who would think you could freeze in Florida?

There were five or maybe six aisles of shelving leading away to the side wall of the building, all of them stacked with more jigsaw puzzles than she'd ever seen before, the box pictures glowing in the glare from the overhead fluorescent lighting.

Megan crossed into the aisle parallel to the one she'd used earlier. There were no boxes stacked here, and she could walk unhindered between the shelves, the pictures of paintings by Da Vinci, Renoir, Monet, and artists she didn't recognize, all surprising in their clarity and richness of detail.

Toward the end of the aisle, the topics changed to images of famous people; presidents, movie stars, and one that caught her eye because of the lack of color. Megan paused by a thousand-piece sepia toned jigsaw of a woman on a white horse. There was a crowd in the background standing before a porticoed building that could be the Capitol building. The woman wore a crown that pushed her long curls back over her shoulders to contrast with the blouse and cloak the same color as the horse.

The title on the box announced Inez Milholland leads the Women's Suffrage March in Washington, DC. March 3, 1913.

Megan frowned and said aloud. "Who was Inez Milholland?" As if in response, the woman lifted her head, turned and fixed her gaze on Megan.

TWO

The first thing Megan felt was tired. A fatigue so bone deep it made her earlier tiredness seem like a burst of energy. For the moment it stilled her fear and terror about what had happened or where she was.

Thankfully, she wasn't on the horse. She was lying on a soft chaise lounge; her head deep in the embrace of a soft cushion, and the comfort almost made her moan with pleasure. It had been losing the silk underwear and thousand thread count sheets that had hurt Megan more than the lack of money.

A firm hand on her left wrist made her forget the fine linens. The man, a doctor Megan assumed, was bent forward, with a frown that wrinkled all the way across his balding head.

"You need to rest, Inez," he said, his voice a low rumble of concern as he placed her hand carefully on her stomach beside the other one. "Your schedule these past weeks has been too much."

Megan felt her head whip forward out of the cushion. Only it wasn't her head. She could see, hear, think, and feel for herself, but she couldn't move without the other woman doing so. And she was aware of everything the other woman felt.

Inez Milholland. The woman in the picture. How in heaven's name did I get here, she wondered. Had she collapsed in the store and this was all a dream?

Megan had to still her thoughts then because Inez was talking. There was such passion and determination in her voice, Megan had no option but to pay attention.

"Rest, doctor? The ladies who come to hear me speak are not ladies of leisure. They are women who've finished a full day's work. Many of them are risking their jobs just to be at Blanchard Hall this evening. Others will sneak away from husbands or fathers. What message does it send about my commitment to Women's Rights if I say I'm too tired to talk to them?"

You go, Megan cheered silently as Inez swung her legs off the chaise, and using her left hand to steady herself, stood carefully because she still couldn't feel her feet.

Inez was at least six inches taller than Megan, and the increase in height gave Megan a new perspective. She enjoyed being at eye level with the doctor and not having to tilt her head up every time she talked to someone.

Inez looked over at the ornate ormolu clock on the mantle, and Megan sensed the woman perform a quick mental calculation. Inez turned to the doctor, his dark suit a contrast to the heavy scarlet drapes edged with gold that covered the windows and kept out the October chill.

"I'll rest for two hours," she said. "Then I will eat. After eating, I will change clothes, and we'll walk to Blanchard Hall for the event. Will that satisfy you, doctor?"

"You need two weeks, or two months, but I suspect two hours is all you'll allow me," he said with a disarming smile.

"Do you have any thoughts on dinner? I'll make sure the hotel has it ready for you."

Megan caught the memory of a meal Inez had eaten in Italy the previous year. She'd been feeling weak and tired then, and the food had given her a new lease of energy.

"Liver and onions," Inez said. "Be sure it's veal liver and marinaded in milk before they cook it."

Megan thought she'd throw up.

The meal wasn't as bad as she expected, although she was certain it was better going into another person's stomach rather than her own. After the meal, Inez went into the equally luxurious bedroom to change. She selected a long black skirt and a crisp white blouse like the one Megan had seen in the jigsaw puzzle.

There were constant interruptions while Inez changed. Other women from the Women's Rights Movement wanted her opinion on wording for posters, questioned the content of her talk, or just wanted to be near her.

By the time they left the hotel to walk the four blocks to Blanchard Hall, Inez was as exhausted as she'd been earlier.

Inez walked out onto the stage. She walked slowly and carefully, her feet numb blocks of weight at the end of her legs. Her mind felt like she was trying to think through a fog, but through that fog Megan could feel her passion, drive, and determination. Inez had spent the past three weeks giving dozens of speeches in eight states. She might be exhausted, but she was going to give these women in Los Angeles her best.

The auditorium wasn't just full. It was overflowing. Megan had overheard one of the other women say the main room at Blanchard Hall seated eight hundred. With the additional people standing in the aisles, along the wall at the back against the dark wood paneling, and peering in through the doorways, Megan estimated there were well over a thousand women waiting impatiently.

The applause and cheering began as Inez stepped out of the wings of the stage and into view. The wall of noise rolled over them. Megan disliked public speaking. A dozen people unnerved her. Ten times that number was terrifying. Her stomach would have been churning with nausea instead of the anticipatory excitement rippling through Inez's body as the bright electric lights highlighted her and followed her to the center of the stage.

"Good evening, Ladies," Inez began, pitching her voice so she could be heard in every corner of the hall. No microphones here, Megan realized. Or teleprompters. Megan felt awed and overwhelmed at what this woman had achieved. She focused as Inez launched into the speech she'd written and memorized.

"The gods of government help those who help themselves. Therefore, women and sisters, and one day fellow voters, let us help ourselves.

"Liberty must be fought for. And, women of the nation, this is the time to fight. This is the time to demonstrate our sisterhood, our spirit, our blithe courage, and our will."

Inez had to pause. The applause and cheering was so loud her words failed to reach the front rows. It had been the same in Seattle, Tacoma, and Spokane.

When the noise subsided, Inez began again. Megan knew the plan was to talk for thirty or forty minutes, then answer questions as she had in San Francisco and Sacramento.

Every few minutes, Inez had to pause, let the noise level subside so her next words could be heard. It reminded Megan of a Kenny Chesney concert she'd attended when she could still afford those things.

Each restart was harder and harder for Inez. Megan felt the force of the other woman's will as physical as the pounding of her heart. Inez had to pause once more, this time for breath as she neared the climax of her speech. She struggled to suck air into her body and lifted her voice again. "Mr. President, how long must women wait for liberty?"

There was more, so much more Inez wanted to tell them, but there was no air in her lungs and the glow of fancy new electric lights in the auditorium faded away. As the darkness overwhelmed them, Megan felt Inez crumple to the hard wooden boards of the stage as the cheers became cries of horror.

THREE

Megan felt the bag slip from her shoulder as she sucked in lungfuls of air and reached for the shelf to steady herself. She twisted her wrist and caught the strap of the bag as it fell. With the bag securely in her hand, she risked another look at the puzzle box.

Inez Milholland looked out of the picture, her eyes fixed on a spot somewhere over the horse's head, not even looking toward Megan. It was just an image. Megan shivered, not sure what had happened to her, but one set of words resonated in her head. *This is the time to demonstrate our courage, and our will.*

There'd been little of that in the past few years, Megan thought as she made her way past more jigsaws. She made a point of not looking at the boxes, and especially not the pictures on the front.

Mac looked up as she came past the counter, the light from the window highlighting the concerned look on his lined face. Like he was worried about her, Megan thought.

"Sit down. I'll get you more coffee," he said, not giving her the chance to argue.

She did as instructed briefly regretting she had to look up

at him when they were both standing. Oddly, Megan felt better than she had in a long time, probably since before she'd started the cleaning job at the motel.

Mac placed the full mug on the table before her.

"Which puzzle was it?" he asked when he was back in his seat.

Megan had just picked up the mug and nearly dropped it.

"There's something about this store," he continued. "Or maybe the land it's on. Most people come in here, browse around, drink some coffee, maybe buy a jigsaw. Occasionally, someone like yourself comes in and afterwards there's something different about them."

"The puzzle was Inez Milholland, the suffragette. How do you know?" Megan was pleased her voice sounded almost normal.

"It happened to me," he said. "You seem to be taking it better than many."

"The last few years have left me with little capacity for surprise," she sipped at the coffee. Courage, Inez had said. "Are you hiring? It looks like you could use some help with those orders."

"It's got a bit out of hand," Mac admitted. He looked at her thoughtfully, his hazel eyes unreadable. "Tell me about yourself."

She hadn't been that open with anyone since the day of Cole's arrest. She took a long swallow of the coffee and a deep breath that pulled the relaxing pine scent of the candle into her body. "I used to be a CPA," she said, and told him everything. Even the incident with Zoe.

"I can't pay much, although I'll pay extra for book-keeping," Mac said when she'd talked herself out. "There's an apartment upstairs. If you cover the utility bills, you can stay there. If you're interested."

Megan nearly dropped the coffee again. Her hands were

shaking, but it wasn't fear or the cold. It was the excitement and anticipation.

"You won't regret it," Megan said, not recognizing her voice until she realized it was from a different Megan.

The Megan who dared.

PIECES OF SILVER

ONE

The brake lights of the cars in front flared bright scarlet in the early evening light. Dan eased his SUV to a stop alongside a green sign with white letters stenciled a foot high and sighed at the long line of brake lights stretching ahead of him to the east. He was two hours early, but the way I-98 was moving, he might be lucky to make it to the restaurant on time.

Making your roads better, the sign said. The Department of Transport signs had been all along I-98 when he was first posted to Eglin a year ago. They were still here, and the only progress he saw was a new set of holes and trenches. Nothing seemed to be finished, and no matter the time of day, there was never anyone working in the construction zone.

He sighed as the traffic edged forward another few feet, wondering not for the first time if he was crazy or stupid or both. Sarah had taken the boys to her parents in Jacksonville, and he'd invited Jessica to have dinner with him. He'd met her in a bar the previous evening after his friends had dragged him out to a seafood and oyster place on the harbor, then they'd gone to the dance floor, which Dan absolutely was not going near.

Jessica had been sitting alone at the bar, blonde hair curling down over her shoulders onto the sleeveless teal silk blouse tucked into her silver pencil skirt. A skirt tight in all the right places.

They'd struck up a conversation. It was refreshing to talk with a woman dressed in something other than sweats and on subjects that didn't revolve around six-year-old twins and elementary school commitments.

Dan had sipped on the one extra drink that made the prospect of the chase energizing and invigorating. He was surprised when she accepted his dinner invitation.

Ahead of him, the traffic moved and kept moving. Now, instead of being late, Dan was going to be embarrassingly early. He couldn't see a coffee shop or diner along the route, but there was a lone building ahead on the right that looked like a restaurant. At a minimum, he could get a coffee.

He'd barely made the conscious decision to check it out when the SUV was bouncing over the low curb and into the gravel parking lot like it had a mind of its own. There was only one other car there, but the building lights were on, so the worst-case scenario was they turned him away because they weren't open.

A bell on the door tinkled softly when Dan pushed it open and stepped inside. He was about to back out when he realized this wasn't a restaurant, but the silver-haired man of about sixty behind the counter was smiling a welcome and the aroma of freshly brewed coffee permeated into every one of Dan's senses.

"Welcome to Puzzle Boutique," the man said. "You look like you could use a coffee. It's fresh, I brewed it not five minutes back."

"I," Dan faltered, looking around. To his left there was an

open area with seating, low tables and several partly completed jigsaw puzzles. To his right and leading back behind the counter were rows of shoulder-high shelving with displays of more jigsaw puzzles than he thought existed.

"You thought this was a restaurant, didn't you," the man said, his smile returning. "It was until a few years ago. The people I bought from turned the place into a specialist store for jigsaw puzzles. I'm Mac. You take cream or sugar in your coffee?" he asked as he poured from the carafe into a pale blue mug.

"Just black," Dan said, wondering about the man's specific phrasing. He accepted the steaming mug, nodded his thanks. "You make a profit doing this?"

"The web presence helps. I'm not as big as those folks up in Missouri, but I make enough to pay the bills and have some left over. I'm probably the only storekeeper on the Gulf Coast who welcomes rainy days during tourist season."

Dan nodded and sipped at the coffee. It was good. Much better than he'd have found in a diner or one of the specialist drive-thrus. "You mind if I look around?"

Mac shook his head. "Be my guest. You have kids?"

"Twin boys. They're six-years old."

"Must have your hands full," Mac said sympathetically. "Start with the children's puzzles over to your right." He waved his hand behind him. "The adult puzzles are everywhere else organized by subject: Christmas, cities, landscapes. You'll get the hang of it. Last count we had about six thousand in stock."

Dan shook his head as he began browsing the children's section, the enormous selection almost bewildering. There were several wood-block puzzles he thought David and Ryan would enjoy, including an F-35 like the one he flew.

He put the F-35 puzzle to one side, added a second one to it, so there'd be no arguments over possession, and wandered deeper into the store. He marveled at the detail and color in the pictures on each box. A wide-angle view of the Trevi Fountain made Dan smile. The picture must have been taken early in the morning because when he'd taken Sarah there, the crowds around the railing were five or six deep.

Another few paces, and Dan was looking at representations of classic Renaissance paintings. Da Vinci's Mona Lisa, and Last Supper, Caravaggio's Taking of Christ. He ambled on, but something made him put the coffee on a nearby shelf and turn back to the Last Supper.

Jesus looked at him.

TWO

It was the smell Dan was aware of first. Unwashed bodies, roasted lamb, and the oil burning in the sconces around the room. The light flickered and flared, making the shadows waltz and pirouette across the walls.

His body felt thinner than he was used to, the cloth of the gray robe rough against his skin and tight across his shoulders. He sat on a stool at the end of the table nearest the door. Jesus was to his left half-way along the table, sitting straight and fingering a cup of wine cradled between both hands.

There were six or seven other disciples between them, dressed in reds, blues and browns, arguing over something Dan couldn't follow. Not that he wanted to. The look of anguish and resignation on Jesus's face transfixed him. A look that made Jesus's cheeks look hollow and sunken.

The mood seemed to go unnoticed among everyone else round the table, even the woman in the cerulean robe whose hand rested familiarly along Jesus's back. He seemed oblivious to the gesture. His head dropped and his fingers tightened on the cup of wine.

When Jesus looked up again, his head turned, and he fixed his dark brown eyes down the table at Dan. "What you are about to do, do quickly."

Dan felt a surge of anger as the body moved with no thought from him. The chair scraped on the floor as he pushed it back and stood. "Yes Rabbi," the sound coming from his body.

"You mean Lord, Judas," said a man at the far end of the table, his head coming up and dark eyes blazing with the quick anger that Dan knew meant this was Peter. The disciple always ready to leap to the defense of his Lord.

"I mean, he is our teacher and to be honored, Peter. I meant no disrespect," Judas said in the soft and humble voice that Dan instinctively knew Judas used to distract the other disciples. Peter scowled and turned back to the conversation he'd been having with his brother Andrew, and James.

Judas hurried out of the room, his sandaled feet slapping noisily on the steep wooden staircase, the money purse bouncing and jingling on his hip. Dan could feel the anger still bubbling inside the man, hear the irate thoughts raging inside Judas's head, all the while wondering how he was here inside this man's head, seeing and hearing everything but unable to say or do anything.

Dan knew the story, knew how it ended, but he didn't know why he was here. He had full use of all five senses but couldn't speak or move unless Judas did so. It was like being inside one of the immersive VR Simulations the scientists were prototyping at Eglin. Except he had no idea how he got here.

As Dan's thoughts alternated from despair and confusion to intrigue, he could feel Judas continue raging in their joined minds.

How could those men be so blind? Scripture predicted the coming of the Messiah. A savior to rid them of the Roman overlords and restore Israel and Judah to the glory they had enjoyed under David and Solomon. This man, Jesus. And he was a man, Judas had no doubt of that. This man Jesus was a powerful teacher, but he was not the Messiah and could not be allowed to continue fostering false hopes among the faithful.

At the bottom of the stairs, Judas stopped and rapped on the door. There was a delay before it creaked open and the innkeeper looked out and glared at Judas.

"What?"

"You want payment as agreed?"

The man wiped food grease from his beard onto the stained sleeve of his robe, his beady black eyes studying Judas. "I charge you an amount and give you back one tenth."

"And one tenth for you," Judas added. "Just make sure the document for me shows that larger amount. What you tell the Roman tax collectors is up to you."

Once the innkeeper was paid, Judas made his way through the streets to the Temple, his mind still reflecting on the meal he had just left.

What sort of Passover celebration was it supposed to be when there was no fourth cup of wine. Judas supposed it made sense because there'd been no recitation of the psalms either. Or a pouring of the fifth cup for Elijah. Jesus had been indulging himself, not celebrating Passover.

The Sanhedrin priest dropped the cloth bag into Judas's hand. The silver coins chinked and rattled noisily in the quiet of the Temple courtyard.

"Thirty pieces, as agreed," the priest said, then whispered almost to himself. "If he really is divine, I wonder what the price is for our lives." Then he realized Judas remained standing before him.

"Still here, Judas? Soldiers of the Temple Guard, and my priests are waiting. You must guide them and make sure they know who he is. I don't want the wrong man arrested. If your Jesus isn't in custody by the end of the night, I'll be expecting you to return the silver."

"He'll be on the Mount of Olives," Judas said. "He's gone there every night this week to pray. If we use the Shushan Gate out of the Temple, it will be much faster."

The group of Temple Guards, priests and servants was larger than Dan expected, or recalled from the days long ago when he'd skimmed the Gospel texts in class. There was an almost festive air in the crowd as they hustled along Solomon's Portico, their excited whispers echoing back from the closely spaced stone columns.

The excitement surprised Dan, given their mission until he felt the same passion and anticipation in every step Judas took. Then it was clear to Dan. For Judas and the priests accompanying him, this was the removal of a threat to their position, not the silencing of a savior. And for Judas, the chance to buy the land he'd coveted for months.

Once through the gate, the ground sloped down into the Kidron Valley. The conversation fell to low murmurs as the party picked their way carefully down the steep narrow rocky path, stones dislodging and clattering away. The soft breeze that had ruffled their hair and played a soft tune in the trees, faded away the lower they got until it died away, and the air was still, with a hint of the chill that reminded Dan winter here had not fully yielded to spring.

"Gethsemane," Judas said in a low voice and pointed ahead and slightly to their left. "He'll be in Gethsemane."

The climb out of the valley wasn't as steep, but the conversation was replaced with huffing and heavy breathing and the occasional muttered curse as a foot caught on a stone or exposed root.

The slope eased and the olive trees became more numerous, their gnarled and twisted trunks taking unnatural shapes in the shadows cast by the full moon in the cloudless starlit sky.

Dan shivered as Judas changed direction, moving to the left and waving for the others to follow him. Ahead of them, Dan saw shapes huddled on the ground, all stirring as a man leaned over them. He heard the voice from the room above the inn, and this time it carried a tone of exasperation.

"Are you still sleeping and taking your rest?"

Dan saw Jesus stiffen as he heard the footfalls of the approaching crowd he turned and saw Judas. "See, the hour is at hand, and the Son of Man is betrayed into the hands of sinners."

As the disciples began stirring and getting to their feet, Judas stepped forward. He kissed Jesus on the cheek and said. "Greetings, Rabbi."

The priests and Temple Guards surged forward, tangling with the disciples. And then Gethsemane was like a brawl site. Fists smacked into flesh, cudgels thudded onto arms and shoulders. Grunts and cries lifted into the tree branches. A raised sword gleamed silver in the moonlight. When it cleaved down, a servant screamed and clutched the side of his head as blood flowed black in the half-light.

"Enough!" Jesus commanded in a voice that seemed to come from all around and deep inside at the same time. There was no denying the order and Dan shivered as Jesus reached out a hand, grabbed Peter's tunic and pulled him back from the brink of a headlong charge. "No more of this." He released Peter, allowing the lack of balance to drop the disciple to the ground.

Jesus reached forward and placed his hand on the servant's head, leaving it there until the blood stopped flowing and the wound healed. Then he turned his attention back to Peter. "Do you think I cannot appeal to my Father and he will at once send twelve legions of Angels. Then how would scripture be fulfilled?"

Peter had no answer. His shoulders sagged and his head dropped. The sword slipped from his fingers, and that was the signal for the soldiers to surge forward and take Jesus into their custody.

As the Guards hustled Jesus away, he turned. His dark eyes burned into Dan's head.

"It's all right, Judas," Jesus said. "You did what you were supposed to do."

One of the priests dragged on Jesus's arm, and the connection between them was broken.

Desolation and emptiness hit Judas and flooded into Dan like something integral to him, something that made him who he was, had been ripped away. He wanted to double over, clutch his belly and wail, but that wasn't an option.

When the first tsunami of emotion faded, the Temple Guard, priests, and servants had gone and Dan found himself alone with the other disciples who looked as devastated as he felt.

"We should stone him," Peter growled, wrestling against the restraining arms of Andrew and Philip who had been holding him back since Peter had dropped his sword.

"Then we're no better than he is, and all our Lord's teaching was for nothing," James said. "Leave him. Let him drown in his own treachery."

As they moved away Simon stepped forward, his face so close, Dan could taste the wine on the other man's breath. "I trusted you," he said, turned away, looked back and spat.

The gob of phlegm hit Dan just below his left eye and as it slid down his cheek, he sank down to the hard earth, the bark of the olive tree scraping his back as the dark empty cloud inside threatened to overwhelm him. The murmur of the disciples' talk faded into the night and all he could hear was the noise of the insects in the branches above him, sounding like a chorus of accusations.

Judas trudged through the nearly empty streets, his head down, hands pushed deep into the sleeves of his robe. His mood was dark, desperate, and desolate. The few other people on the streets this early seemed to sense the darkness and moved away. Even the Roman soldiers guarding the Tekoa Gate made no comment or attempt to stop him.

The sun was just coloring the eastern horizon when Judas stopped walking and stood for a moment surveying the land before him. It was a field with no grass or other vegetation, just a few bare olive trees and ridges of red clay pitted with holes and shallow trenches where the pot makers had dug for their raw materials.

The Potter's Field, Dan remembered. The land Judas purchased with the silver he'd received for betraying Jesus.

And as Judas walked toward the nearest olive tree uncoiling the length of rope from his shoulder, Dan remembered the other role this field played in the life of Judas.

"No! You can't," Dan tried to yell even though he knew Judas could not hear him. The man was consumed with guilt, and there was nothing and no-one to whom he could offer repentance. The thoughts were loud in Dan's mind. For Judas there was no redemption. Nothing he did would ever restore the trust and respect of the disciples or any other person.

"Forgive me, Lord Jesus," Judas said, as he let himself fall from the branch, the rope jerking tight round his throat.

As the last of life choked out of Judas, and everything went dark, Dan understood.

THREE

Dan stumbled against the shelving, gasping for air, his mind still swirling at what he'd experienced and the message it left him with. He steadied himself and rearranged the puzzle boxes he'd displaced or knocked over. The mug was where he'd left it, steam still rising, and when his shaking hand picked up the mug, the coffee was still hot.

Shakily, he made his way back to the front of the store.

"See anything you liked?" Mac asked.

"How long was I in there?"

"About five minutes. Maybe ten," Mac gave him a knowing smile that lit up his hazel eyes. "I wondered if something would happen. You had that look about you when you came in. Which puzzle was it?"

"The Last Supper," Dan answered automatically.

Mac's hazel eyes went wide, and he said thoughtfully. "That's a new one. I need to make a note of that."

"This has happened before?"

"It happens," Mac refilled his own mug and led Dan over to the lounge chairs. "I've had the store for nearly two years, he said when they were comfortable. "It's taken a while, but now I recognize those who are searching for something."

"I'm not. I wasn't."

"You intended to come into a puzzle store?" Mac asked with a raised eyebrow and a disarming smile.

"Not at all. I told you I was early for an appointment and wanted to kill some time, and," Dan paused. "And maybe I was looking for some type of displacement activity."

"And now?"

Dan shrugged. He wasn't sure, and he couldn't put it in words. Not yet, anyway.

"Sometimes it takes a while to sort it out," Mac said getting up. He crossed to the counter and poured coffee into a tall takeout cup. He handed it to Dan with a smile. "Take some coffee with you. I have a feeling you might need it."

"How does it work?" Dan asked, accepting the tall polystyrene container. "The puzzles."

"It's a puzzle. And pun intended," Mac said. "I have no idea. Having experienced it myself, I know what happens, but I have no idea how or why. Maybe we should just be thankful something or someone wants to reset our path."

Outside, the sun had set and the last orange light of day had changed to a fading salmon-pink as Dan climbed back into the SUV. He started the engine, reached for his phone and sent a text: *Had a crisis come out of the blue. Afraid I won't make it.*

He didn't expect a reply and was surprised when his phone tinged before he reached the parking lot exit. He braked and read the message.

No problem. I'm chatting with a hunky Marine from Pensacola.

Dan leaned back against the leather bucket seat, catching his reflection in the windshield, the twist of a smile on his face. Wasn't that just like the Marines? And a sure sign of what he might have gotten himself into. After a moment, he sipped at the coffee and punched coordinates into the navigation system.

"Five hours and three minutes to your destination," Siri told him.

As he accelerated out of the lot, Dan wondered if he could shave thirty or forty minutes off that time heading east to Jacksonville on I-10. It was down to him to expand the conversation, but right now, Dan really wanted to spend time with sweats and pre-school discussions.

ABOUT THE AUTHOR

Richard Freeborn has consulted in health care software since coming to the US from England nearly thirty years ago. He lives in Auburn, Alabama with his wife, two dogs, and one cat. All of whom occasionally let him think he runs the house.

Richard writes in many different genres. His website is www.richardfreeborn.com.

ALSO BY RICHARD FREEBORN

Thieves in the Temple

Jacob fought desperately to save Jerusalem from the Babylonian invaders. Injured and exiled, Jacob builds a new life among his former enemies in the city of Babylon.

As the Babylonians celebrate their New Year, Jacob uncovers a conspiracy threatening the freedom and lives of every one of the Exiles.

Uncertain who to trust Jacob unravels the threads of deceit into a compelling climax that saves not just the Exiles, but Jacob himself.

Get Thieves in the Temple here: **https://books2read.com/u/47lWOA**

www.ingramcontent.com/pod-product-compliance
Lightning Source LLC
LaVergne TN
LVHW020652100826
845148LV00012B/2447

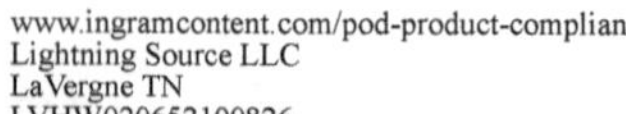

* 9 7 8 0 9 7 5 2 7 9 1 3 7 *